DUCK'S BREATH
— AND —
MOUSE PIE

A Collection of Animal Superstitions
by Steve Jenkins

Ticknor & Fields Books for Young Readers
New York 1994

Published by
Ticknor & Fields Books for Young Readers
A Houghton Mifflin company, 215 Park Avenue South, New York, New York 10003

Manufactured in the United States of America

Book design by Steve Jenkins
The text of this book is set in 14 point Bauer Bodoni
The illustrations are paper collage, reproduced in full color

BVG 10 9 8 7 6 5 4 3 2 1

Library of Congress Cataloging-in-Publication Data
Jenkins, Steve.
Duck's breath and mouse pie: a collection of animal superstitions / by Steve Jenkins
Includes bibliographic references. p. cm.
ISBN 0-395-69688-7
1. Animals—Folklore—Juvenile literature. 2. Superstitions—Juvenile literature.
[1. Animals—Folklore. 2. Folklore. 3. Superstition.]
I. Title. II. Title: Duck's breath and mouse pie.
GR705.J46 1994
398.24'5—dc20   94-2499   CIP AC

For Alec and Page

A wish made upon seeing
the first frog in spring
will come true.

A
peacock
feather
in the
house
brings
bad
luck.

To cure a sick child,

pass the child three times

under the belly of a donkey.

A black cat crossing your path is bad luck.

Toads can
cure illness
and remove
curses.

It is lucky to see a dalmatian.

A cock
crowing at
night foretells
bad luck.

Tie
a beetle
to a thread
around a child's
neck to cure
whooping
cough.

If a stork
nests on
a roof,
a baby
will be
born in
that house.

A bumblebee in the house means a visitor will come.

If a
shark
follows
a ship, there
will be a death on board.

To cure an
illness, place
a live duck's
bill in the
sick person's
mouth.

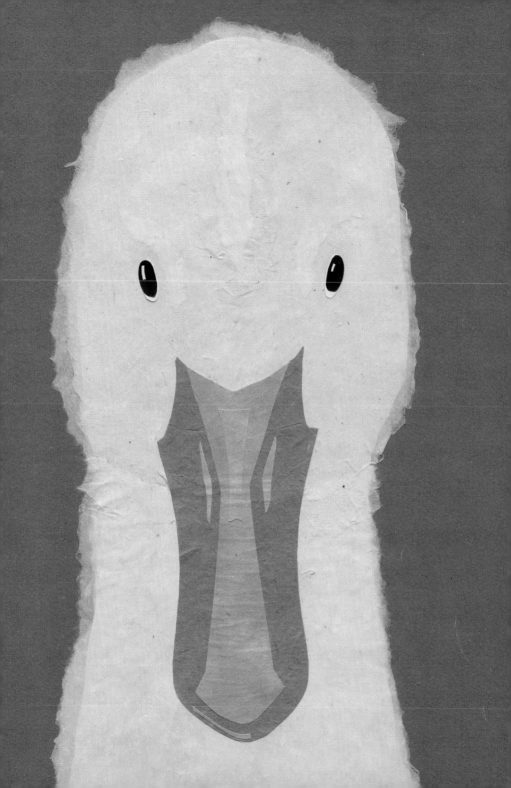

A snail's track will spell your future sweetheart's initials.

Throw a hairy caterpillar over your left shoulder for good luck.

Drink milk in which a fish has been swimming to cure whooping cough.

A
lizard
entering
your
house
means
you will
have
bad
luck.

A
mouse
eaten in
a pie will
cure stuttering.

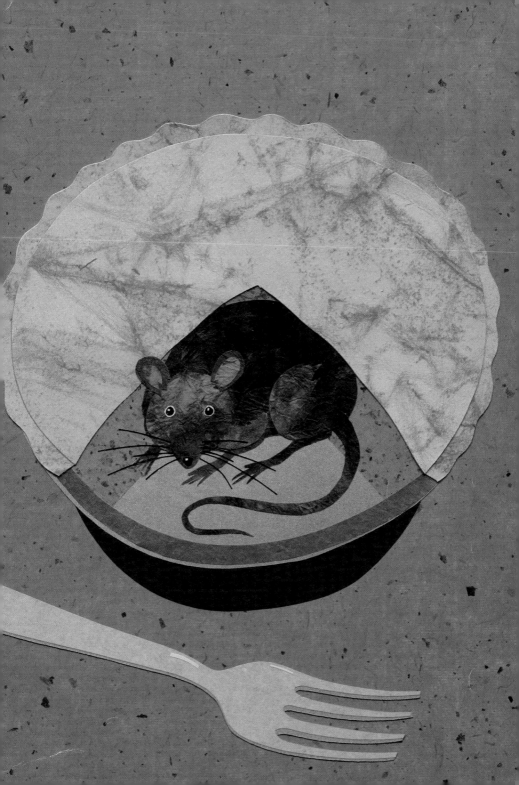

Throughout history, most people lived in close contact with the natural world. They grew or caught their food, and their lives were dependent on the seasons and the weather. Daily life was often hazardous, and disease and natural disaster were constant threats.

People looked for ways to explain the good and bad things that happened to them. They attempted to cure illnesses, even when the causes of diseases were unknown, and they tried to find out or influence what the future might bring. People came to believe that there was meaning hidden within many of the ordinary and extraordinary events of their lives. These beliefs are called superstitions.

The superstitions in this book are old, and most of them seem strange to us today. A sick child is more likely to visit a doctor than to be passed under the belly of a donkey. Yet modern science has not made superstitions disappear. When people fear that walking under a ladder will cause bad luck or wear their "lucky shirt" to try out for the baseball team, they are attempting to control their destiny just as people have in the past.

The origin of a specific superstition is not always known, not even by people who believe it. Someone might avoid black cats without knowing why they are considered bad luck. Still, it is sometimes possible to discover why an old superstition was believed, because superstitions reflect people's understanding of the world around them.

A wish made upon seeing the first frog in spring will come true.

This belief probably has its origins in the importance of spring for farmers and others whose livelihood depends on the seasons. Frogs appear only after the ground has warmed up and planting can begin. Other creatures also bring good luck when first sighted: hairy caterpillars, butterflies, and swallows. These, too, are signs of spring's arrival.

The first appearance of something is still considered a time to make a wish, as when we say "Star light, star bright, /First star I see tonight/I wish I may, I wish I might/Have the wish I wish tonight."

A peacock feather in the house brings bad luck.

The bright colors of a peacock's feather do not fade when the peacock dies. That is why, many hundreds of years ago, these feathers were symbols of immortality. Later, peacock feathers were used as decorations at funerals and they became associated with death, especially in England in the 1800s. (Of course, that does not mean that everyone in England believed this superstition, only that some people did.)

There may be another reason for this superstition. The pattern on the peacock's tail feathers looks like eyes. Some people said they were "evil eyes"—eyes that the devil could spy through.

To cure a sick child, pass the child three times under the
belly of a donkey.

People used to believe that a donkey would go off by itself when it was about to die. "You'll never see a dead donkey," people said, and so donkeys were associated with life. In Ireland, people believed that donkeys were lucky and would protect children because a donkey was present when Jesus Christ was born. The sick child would be passed three times under (or under and over) the animal because three has for centuries been considered a lucky number.

In the past, a folk cure like this one sometimes gave patients a better chance of recovering than a doctor's medicine would. A doctor might take large amounts of blood every day, which weakened the patient, or prescribe medicines containing mercury or other poisons. Folk healers used herbs (some of which had healing qualitities) or magical cures, which usually did no harm and allowed the patient's body to try to heal itself.

A black cat crossing your path is bad luck.

This is the best-known animal superstition. For thousands of years, the black cat has been a symbol of magic, witchcraft, and the evil forces of the night. Black cats accompanied underworld gods in both Greek and Scandinavian mythology. In English and American folklore, black cats have long been associated with witches. The cat was the companion of the witches—or even the witch herself, in disguise.

Superstitions vary from time to time and from place to place. In Scotland, encountering a black cat is thought to bring good luck.

Toads can cure illness and remove curses.

The toad's unusual appearance—lumpy, with jewel-like eyes—makes it interesting to people. Some say that touching a toad will cause warts (another superstition), but in the past the toad was respected. Toads were allowed to live in people's houses, probably because they ate flies and other insects.

An English superstition, popular from the fifteenth to the nineteenth centuries, said that one of the lumps on a toad's head contained a special stone called a toadstone. This stone was said to possess many wonderful qualities, including the ability to cure illness, relieve the pain of insect stings or snake bites, remove evil spells and curses, and change color in the presence of poisons. The toadstone had to be given freely by the toad, not taken from it, if the magic was to work. One way to encourage a toad to eject its stone was to place it on fabric of its favorite color: scarlet.

It is lucky to see a dalmatian.

Dalmatians, like many other dogs, can perform a variety of tasks, but for centuries they have been famous for their ability to work with horses and horse-drawn vehicles. English royalty in particular liked dalmatians and used them to accompany their carriages. The dogs would either clear a path for the team of horses or follow the coach. Their association with royalty and the belief that it was lucky to associate with those who, like the aristocracy, were fortunate themselves, may have suggested to people that these dogs signified good fortune.

A cock crowing at night foretells bad luck.

The rooster's cry announces the end of night and the coming of the dawn, and is a good omen. But if the rooster crows in the middle of the night, something is wrong in the natural order of things— generally a sign of trouble. This belief was recorded almost two thousand years ago by the Latin writer Petronius.

Tie a beetle to a thread around a child's neck to cure whooping cough.

Many folk cures involve attaching a living animal to the sick person. People believed that as the animal died and decayed, the illness was transferred to it, and the patient would be healed.

The beetle appears in many superstitions and folktales. The belief in its power to cure illness, cause good or bad luck, or change the weather may be related to the beetle's mysterious life underground.

Pliny, the famous Roman naturalist, mentions this belief almost two thousand years ago, and people in England knew about it in the 1800s.

If a stork nests on a roof, a baby will be born in that house.

Storks are common birds in many cities in Northern Europe. They have long been known for their devotion to their mates and offspring. They also return each spring to the same house, where they build nests on roofs and chimneys. The superstition connecting storks and newborn babies may result from the storks' appearance in spring, a season traditionally associated with birth—and with parents' reluctance to explain to their children where the new baby really came from. It is harder to explain why this belief was popular in England, where there are no storks. Even in the United States, pictures of storks still appear on birth announcements.

A bumblebee in the house means a visitor will come.

Since ancient times, people have thought bees were divine messengers or could foretell the future. Bees were important. They provided honey—which was especially valued before sugar became available—and beeswax, which was made into candles. People treated bees as the friends and protectors of a household, and, in England, the bees in a family's hive had to be told important news, especially of a death in the family. Otherwise, they might take offense and fly away.

Many superstitions come from people's finding significance in unusual events. The house was an unusual place to find a bumblebee, and because the bee was a friend, its appearance foretold something pleasant: the arrival of a visitor.

If a shark follows a ship, there will be a death on board.

It was once widely believed certain animals had the ability, through their keen sense of smell, to know if someone was about to die. Sharks can smell blood in the water from a long way off. Sailors believed that the shark could smell a death before it occurred.

To cure an illness, place a live duck's bill in the sick person's mouth.

Before diseases were understood, people believed that many illnesses were carried by the air. This, of course, is not entirely wrong, but it resulted in such unsound practices as keeping sick people for long periods in rooms with all the windows tightly closed. The duck's purpose, in this belief from western England, was to breathe in the illness, drawing it away from the sick person and into itself. The Irish had a similar superstition, but they used a goose's bill instead.

A snail's track will spell your future sweetheart's initials.

People look for meaning in any random, complex scene. Some people believe that the pattern left by tea leaves in the bottom of a cup will tell them their future.

A snail's meandering leaves behind a distinctive shiny track, so it is easy to imagine that letters of special significance are being spelled out. Sometimes the snail was set on a surface spread with ashes or flour, making the trail easier to see. This belief was reported in England and Ireland, as early as 1714 and as late as 1957.

Throw a hairy caterpillar over your left shoulder for good luck.

Its transformation into a butterfly or moth and its association with spring made the caterpillar interesting and noteworthy. Other things, such as salt, are also thrown over the *left* shoulder for luck, or to avoid bad luck, because that is considered throwing it into the devil's face.

Drink milk in which a fish has been swimming to cure whooping cough.

There are many beliefs concerning fish, most of which come from people who live near the sea. Fish have long been symbols of life and strength. They are also thought to have many magical and curative powers, perhaps because they live underwater, in a mysterious world inaccessible to people.

A lizard entering your house means you will have bad luck.

Many folktales and legends, as well as the Bible, associate snakes, dragons, and lizards with the devil or other evil forces. The appearance of a reptile in a place it should not be and did not usually go suggested that something bad was going to happen.

A mouse eaten in a pie will cure stuttering.

Not only stuttering, but colds, measles, and bedwetting were treated by eating mice—fried, roasted, burned and ground up, or in a pie. It is difficult to understand why this was believed to help. Mice were known to spread disease, and it may be that eating them was considered a kind of vaccination, similar to being protected against polio or flu by taking tiny amounts of the organism that caused the disease—but that theory still does not explain why they would cure bedwetting or stuttering. Nevertheless, this belief was reported by the Roman naturalist Pliny in A.D. 77, and has been recorded in England since the sixteenth century.

Bibliography

Ferm, Vergilius Ture Anselm. *A Brief Dictionary of American Superstitions*. New York: Philosophical Library, 1959.

Haining, Peter. *Superstitions*. London: Sidgewick & Jackson, 1979.

Koch, William E. *Folklore from Kansas: Customs, Beliefs, and Superstitions*. Lawrence, Kans.: Regents Press of Kansas, 1980.

Laing, Jeanie M. *Notes on Superstition and Folk Lore*. 1885. Norwood, Pa.: Norwood Editions, 1973.

Lorie, Peter. *Superstitions*. New York: Simon & Schuster, 1992.

Opie, Iona and Moira Tatem, eds. *Dictionary of Superstitions*. Oxford: Oxford University Press, 1989.

Radford, E. and M. A. Radford. *Encyclopaedia of Superstitions*. 1949. Reprint. Westport, Conn.: Greenwood Press, 1973.